ENGINEERING SUPER STRUCTURES

BRIDGES

PAIGE V. POLINSKY

Consulting Editor, Diane Craig, M.A./Reading Specialist

Sandcastle

An Imprint of Abdo Publishing
abdopublishing.com

abdopublishing.com

Published by Abdo Publishing, a division of ABDO, PO Box 398166, Minneapolis, Minnesota 55439. Copyright © 2018 by Abdo Consulting Group, Inc. International copyrights reserved in all countries. No part of this book may be reproduced in any form without written permission from the publisher. SandCastle™ is a trademark and logo of Abdo Publishing.

Printed in the United States of America, North Mankato, Minnesota

062017
092017

THIS BOOK CONTAINS
RECYCLED MATERIALS

Design: Kelly Doudna, Mighty Media, Inc.
Production: Mighty Media, Inc.
Editor: Rebecca Felix
Cover Photographs: Mighty Media, Inc.; Shutterstock
Interior Photographs: iStockphoto, Shutterstock

Publisher's Cataloging-in-Publication Data

Names: Polinsky, Paige V., author.
Title: Bridges / by Paige V. Polinsky.
Description: Minneapolis, MN : Abdo Publishing, 2018. | Series: Engineering
    super structures.
Identifiers: LCCN 2016962860 | ISBN 9781532111013 (lib. bdg.) |
    ISBN 9781680788860 (ebook)
Subjects: LCSH: Bridges--Juvenile literature. | Bridges--Design and construction--
    Juvenile literature. | Civil engineering--Juvenile literature.
Classification: DDC 624--dc23
LC record available at http://lccn.loc.gov/2016962860

SandCastle™ Level: Fluent

SandCastle™ books are created by a team of professional educators, reading specialists, and content developers around five essential components—phonemic awareness, phonics, vocabulary, text comprehension, and fluency—to assist young readers as they develop reading skills and strategies and increase their general knowledge. All books are written, reviewed, and leveled for guided reading, early reading intervention, and Accelerated Reader™ programs for use in shared, guided, and independent reading and writing activities to support a balanced approach to literacy instruction. The SandCastle™ series has four levels that correspond to early literacy development. The levels are provided to help teachers and parents select appropriate books for young readers.

EMERGING • BEGINNING • TRANSITIONAL • FLUENT

CONTENTS

About Bridges

Bridges create paths over
obstacles.

Many reach across rivers.

Early bridges were simple. Ancient humans used logs to cross streams.

People later
built stone
bridges.

Today, many
bridges are **steel**.

8

Others are **concrete**. There are
more than 500,000 bridges in
the United States.

Trains use bridges to cross rivers.
They cross **canyons** on bridges too.

Trains carry
goods across
the country.

Cars also travel on bridges.
Some bridges have bike paths.

There are different types of
bridges. Truss bridges have
triangular frames.

Cable-stayed bridges use cables to **support** roads.

The Golden Gate Bridge is a suspension bridge. It is in California.

It is 1.7 miles
(2.7 km) long.

Bridges **support**
a lot of weight.

Engineers must make
them very strong.

Engineers visit bridges often.
They look for and fix **damage**.

With the right care,
a bridge can last
hundreds of years!

Think About It

Bridges help you cross rivers. What else might a bridge help you cross?

With the right care,
a bridge can last
hundreds of years!

Think About It

Bridges help you cross rivers. What else might a bridge help you cross?

GLOSSARY

canyon – a deep, narrow valley between two cliffs.

concrete – a mixture of sand, gravel, cement, and water that becomes hard when it dries.

damage – harm or ruin.

engineer – someone who is trained to design and build structures such as machines, cars, or roads.

obstacle – something that you have to go over or around.

steel – a strong, hard metal made from iron.

support – to hold up.